THE CARS

ELLIOT   DAVID   RIC   BEN   GREG

BY
Robus Productions

robus books

P.O. Box 13819 • Wauwatosa, WI 53213 U.S.A.

ISBN 0-88188-364-6

Text by Stacy Leigh
Photography by Mike O'Brien and Kelly Thompson

1976

Songwriting and performing partners for almost a decade before The Cars were assembled, Richard (Ric) Ocasek and Benjamin (Ben) Orzechowski (Orr) had worked together in bands in Cleveland, Ohio, New York City, Woodstock, N.Y. and Ann Arbor, Mich., before settling in Cambridge, Mass. in 1976.

That year Ocasek and Orr re-established a working relationship with keyboardist Greg Hawkes. They'd met six years earlier, when Hawkes, then a session musician, played on an album by the folk group Milkwood, which Ocasek and Orr had fronted.

Guitarist Elliot Easton, who'd been a part of Ocasek's and Orr's popular Boston-based band Cap'n Swing in 1974, and ex-Modern Lovers/DMZ drummer David Robinson were also recruited—and The Cars were underway.

The name, Easton says, was chosen because it meant nothing in particular, but provided endless possibilities for catchy headlines— possibilities which the press seized on immediately.

BEN

The name was chosen because it meant nothing in particular, but provided endless possibilities for catchy headlines.

1977

The Cars quickly earned a sizeable reputation in the Boston area. By mid-1977 they'd headlined dates in every major club and opened shows for Bob Seger, J. Geils, Nils Lofgren and Foreigner. A demo of "Just What I Needed" became the most requested track on top-rating Boston radio stations WCOZ-FM and WBCN-FM.

From the scattered and mostly fruitless experimenting with synthesized pop styles that characterized American New Wave in the late 1970s, The Cars emerged as the first home-grown band to have a recognizable commercial impact and a sound all its own. Their flat, monochromatic vocals, their clipped, precise rhythms, their fascination with alienation and minimalist repetition brought The Cars to the leading edge of the new pop sensibility. Yet Hawkes' bright synthesizer slashes and Easton's intricate, countrified guitar flourishes rooted them to classic American rock.

By the end of the year The Cars had signed with Elektra Records and made plans to record their debut LP.

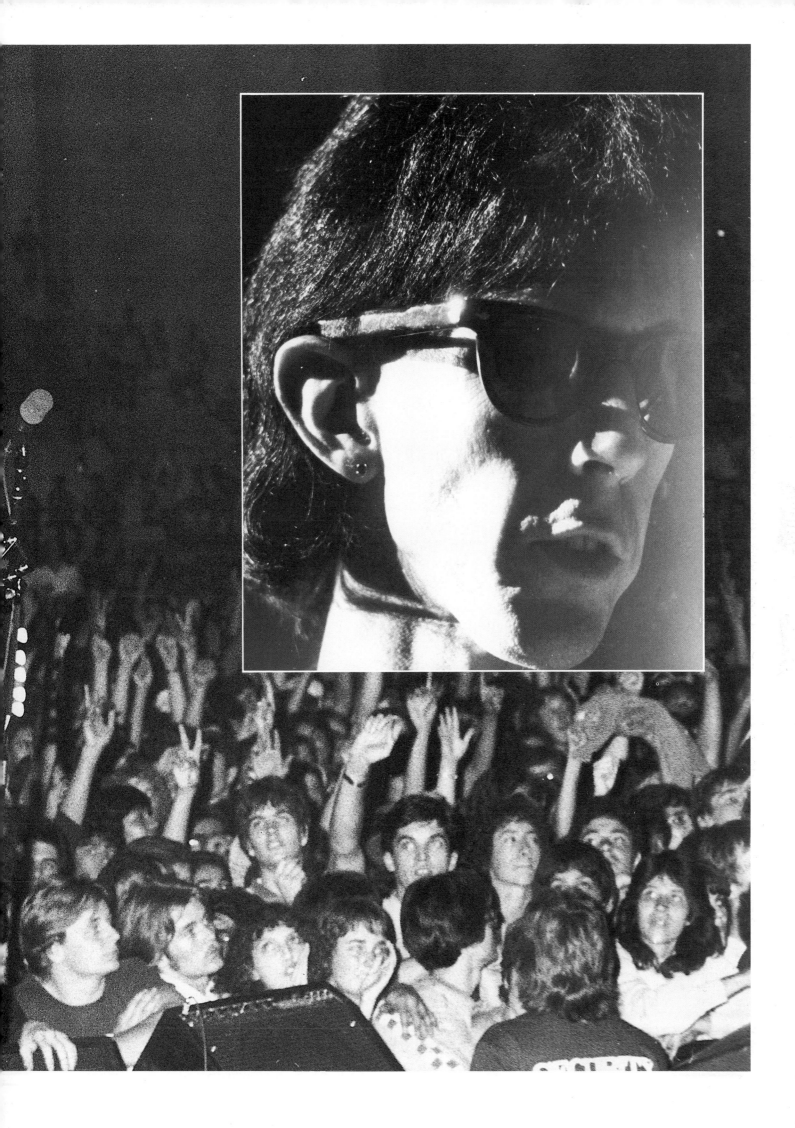

1978

With veteran producer Roy Thomas Baker (Queen), The Cars recorded their first album—self-titled—in London in just two weeks. It was released in May, and yielded three hit singles—"Just What I Needed," "My Best Friend's Girl" and "Good Times Roll."

So overwhelming was the impact The Cars had on American music in 1978 that they were named *Rolling Stone* magazine's Band Of The Year. Their expressionless faces adorned the covers of tabloids and fanzines around the world. Ocasek and Orr were seen as hip prophets of a new era of American rock supremacy, one in which technological sophistication, musical simplicity and sound songwriting craftsmanship would break new ground.

1979

By the middle of this year The Cars had begun headlining their own shows in arenas across North America. Reviews emphasized the band's coldness on stage, its inaccessibility. The Cars weren't pop stars in the classic mold; and their performances deliberately questioned the values of bombastic American rockers of the 1970s, stylists and technicians who seemed content to restate what had come before.

The success of The Cars debut had proven America was responding again to innovation. The release of **Candy-O**, the band's second album, was delayed till mid-June because of the durability of its predecessor. "Good Times Roll", the third Top 20 single from **The Cars**, was still high in the charts when "Let's Go", **Candy-O**'s first single, began its rise.

If the band's live performances left something to be desired, its recordings seemed irresistible. In the following year, **The Cars** and **Candy-O** would sell 6,000,000 copies between them.

Late in 1979 The Cars hosted a segment of the popular Midnight Special TV rock series—and introduced the bleak, nihilist Boston duo Suicide, whom Ocasek would later produce.

In 1978 they were named Rolling Stone *magazine's Band of The Year.*

1980

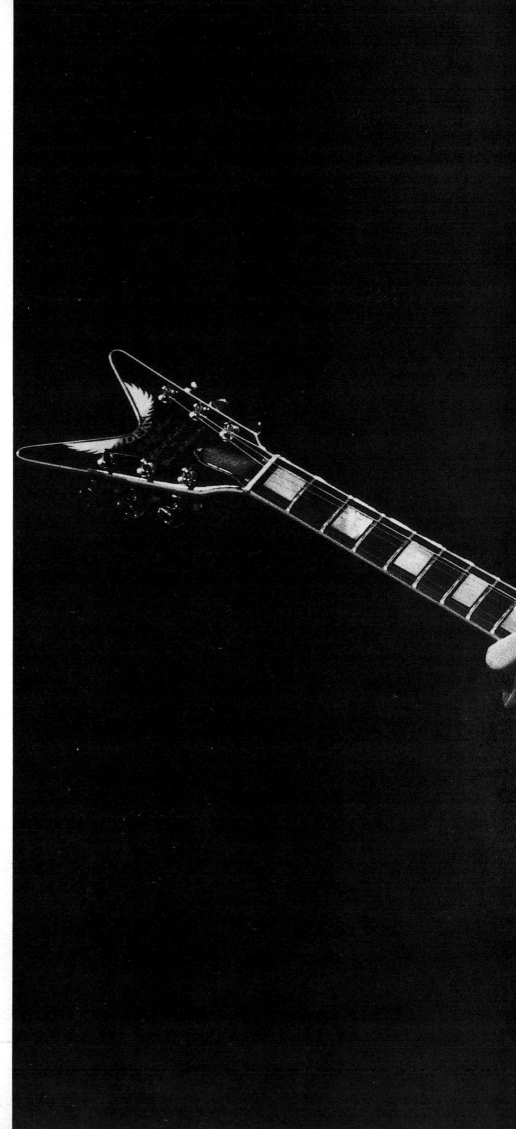

Having established a substantial track record, The Cars departed from the norm with their 1980 LP, **Panorama**, which was in no small part influenced by the emerging British art-rock movement and by Ocasek's obsession with lyrical minimalism and musical dissonance. **Panorama** was a far less successful LP for the band, though it did spawn one platinum hit—"Touch And Go."

Cars fans seemed to prefer the relatively safer territory of **Candy-O**, which achieved platinum status in 1980, and **The Cars**, which still lingered on the charts two years after its release.

*The Cars emerged as the first home-grown
band to have a recognizable commercial
impact and a sound all its own.*

In 1980 "The Cars" and "Candy-O" sold 6,000,000 copies between them.

1981

Though **Panorama** achieved a satisfactory 1,000,000 sales, The Cars seemed shaky through 1981. Everyone in the band had embarked on solo ventures, either recording alone or producing underground acts that lingered on the fringes of acceptable pop. Ocasek finished the Suicide (Alan Vega and Martin Rev) album he'd begun a year before, and produced singles and EPs for Boston's New Models, for the Peter Dayton Band, for pop courtesan Bebe Buell and for San Francisco's Romeo Void.

David Robinson produced singles for The Vinny Band and for Boys Life, while Easton completed a project with The Dawgs.

Having secured its own niche, members of the band rationalized it was time to spread their good fortune among other struggling acts, acts who'd chosen, as The Cars once had, to challenge the musical status quo.

As it turned out, their reach exceeded their grasp; only Romeo Void had any degree of success.

Despite the apparent dissolution, The Cars used this year to consolidate. They bought their own studio, Syncro Sound, in Boston and recorded parts of 1981's **Shake It Up** LP there, again with producer Roy Thomas Baker. The title track and "Victim Of Love" were both reasonable hits in following months.

DISCOGRAPHY

ALBUMS:

The Cars (Elektra 6E-135, 1978): Good Times Roll, My Best Friend's Girl, Just What I Needed, I'm In Touch With Your World, Don't Cha Stop, You're All I've Got Tonight, Bye Bye Love, Moving In Stereo, All Mixed Up.

Candy-O (Elektra 5E-507, 1979): Let's Go, Since I Held You, It's All I Can Do, Double Life, Shoo Be Doo, Candy-O, Night Spots, You Can't Hold On Too Long, Lust For Kicks, Got A Lot On My Head, Dangerous Type.

Panorama (Elektra 54-514, 1980): Panorama, Touch And Go, Gimme Some Slack, Don't Tell Me No, Getting Through, Misfit Kid, Down Boy, You Wear Those Eyes, Running To You, Up And Down.

Shake It Up (Elektra 54-567, 1981): Since You're Gone, Shake It Up, I'm Not The One, Victim Of Love, Cruiser, A Dream Away, This Could Be Love, Think It Over, Maybe Baby.

Heartbeat City (Elektra 60-296, 1984): Hello Again, Looking For Love, Magic, Drive, Stranger Eyes, You Might Think, It's Not The Night, Why Can't I Have You, I Refuse, Heartbeat City.

SINGLES:
Just What I Needed (May, 1978); My Best Friend's Girl (October, 1978); Good Times Roll (February, 1979); Let's Go (June, 1979); It's All I Can Do (September, 1979); Double Life (December, 1979); Touch And Go (August, 1980); Don't Tell Me No (November, 1980); Gimme Some Slack (January, 1981); Shake It Up (November, 1981); Since You're Gone (March, 1982); You Might Think (March, 1984).

HOW TO CONTACT THE CARS

In U.S.A.,
℅ Elektra/Asylum Records,
665 Fifth Ave.,
New York, N.Y. 10022 U.S.A.

In U.K.,
℅ WEA Records,
20 Broadwick St.,
London W1A 2BH, England.

ELLIOT

DAVID

GREG

1984

Between 1982 and this year, Ocasek, Hawkes and Orr all released solo albums that failed to measure up to The Cars' standard, though each LP contained elements of the band's unique style. Easton (The Peter Bond Set and Jules Shear) and Ocasek (Bad Brains) continued producing for others, but it appeared that their enthusiasm for The Cars had waned.

Heartbeat City, released in March 1984, proved otherwise. Boosted by the phenomenal computer-generated video for "You Might Think"—which won first prize in the First International Music Video Festival in St. Tropez in October 1984—**Heartbeat City** was The Cars' best-selling LP since their debut, with sales nudging double platinum. And it yielded three more Top 20 hits—"Magic," "Drive" and "Hello Again".

Freed by video from what Ocasek once referred to as "the discomfort of performing" on stage, The Cars are once again in the vanguard of new American rock, embracing a new sense of adventure and propelled by a new energy.

*In October 1984 the computer-generated
video for "You Might Think" won first prize
in the First International Music Video
Festival.*